GRIMM

AND

GROSS

Raintree is an imprint of Capstone Global Library Limited, a company incorporated in England and Wales having its registered office at 264 Banbury Road, Oxford, OX2 7DY – Registered company number: 6695582

www.raintree.co.uk
myorders@raintree.co.uk

Edited by Eliza Leahy
Designed by Bob Lentz
Original illustrations © Capstone Global Library Limited 2019
Production by Tori Abraham
Originated by Capstone Global Library Ltd
Printed and bound in India

ISBN 978 1 4747 6747 7
22 21 20 19 18
10 9 8 7 6 5 4 3 2 1

British Library Cataloguing in Publication Data
A full catalogue record for this book is available from the British Library.

THE WOLF
AND THE
SEVEN KIDS

A GRIMM AND GROSS RETELLING

BY BENJAMIN HARPER
ILLUSTRATED BY TIMOTHY BANKS

raintree

a Capstone company — publishers for children

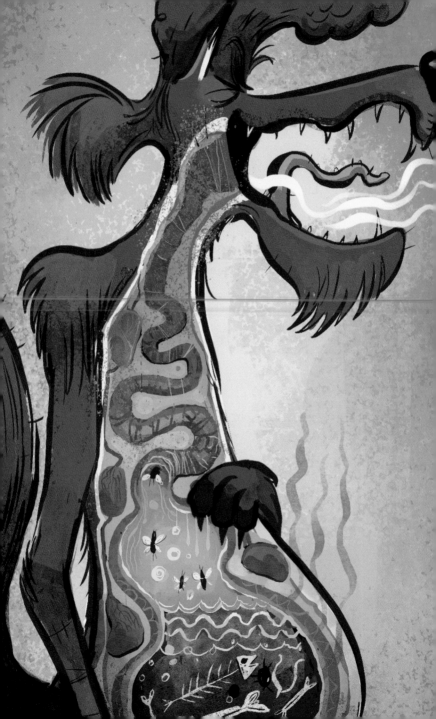

CONTENTS

WARNING!

You might need a strong stomach for this story.

The wolf needs one too, but it doesn't matter.

His gastric problems start when he's asleep.

The story is gross enough when you read what

those little kids use for toppings on their pizza.

But what they do to the wolf – yuck!

Nothing tops that!

GRIM

The Grimm brothers were known for writing some *GRIM* tales. Look for the thumbs-down and you'll know the story is about to get grim.

GROSS

Luckily there's also a lot of *GROSS* stuff in this story. Look for the thumbs-up to see when it's about to get gross.

---

1. These are footnotes. Get it? Dr Grossius Grimbus, researcher of all things grim and gross, shares his highly scientific observations.

CHAPTER ONE
TERROR IN MUSHROOM GROVE

The tiny town of Mushroom Grove sat on the edge of a deep, dark, scary forest. It was a terrifying time in this once-peaceful village. Citizens had been disappearing.

"*SQUEEEEEAL!*" the three pigs cried. "It was the wolf!" These pigs knew what they were talking about. Last year the wolf had blown down two of their houses trying to eat them! But the town's police hadn't been able to catch anyone connected to the strange disappearances. There were no clues to be found anywhere. Children were warned to stick together. Most importantly, they were told to stay far, far away from the forest. Dangers surely lurked therein!

In spite of everything going on, the townsfolk tried to stay happy. They all went about their normal business. The Cow family still held its annual car wash to raise money for milk awareness. Mr and Mrs Goose kept making their world-famous apple butter. The children still went to school and played in the park.

On the outskirts of Mushroom Grove over at Mrs Goat's house, the town's troubles were far from everyone's minds.

"Pizza party!" Mikey Goat bleated. His six brothers and sisters all jumped up and down.

Today was Mikey's birthday. His mother had promised them all a special dinner to celebrate. But she had just received a call that the pizza delivery chicken's car had broken down. She would have to go into town to pick up the pizzas.

"Oh dear," Mrs Goat sighed, putting her

phone down. She worried about leaving her children alone in the house. After all, the dark forest bordered their back garden. And lately, the kids had seen strange shadows moving among the trees. Mrs Goat called the children over.

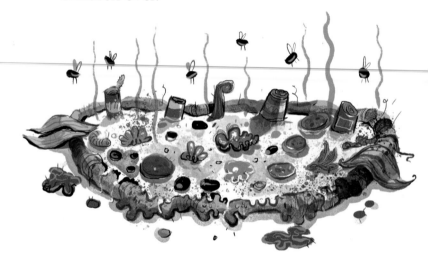

"Now listen up," she said. "I have to go and get the pizzas. And, yes, I got rotten egg, wilted lettuce, tin can and a large Rubbish Special, complete with tissues, old jumper and expired pepperoni," she said before all the goats chimed in with their favourite toppings.[1] "I want you all to stay inside this house. Don't open the door for anyone. If it's the wolf who's behind these disappearances, he'll eat you all up!" She paused. "Remember what we learned from Red Riding Hood. He'll try to disguise himself, but you'll know it's him by his black paws and his deep voice."

"Mum, hurry up before that rotten egg gets cold," Tina said.

"I can't wait to eat that recycled bacon grease! It adds just the right touch," Alexander added.

"Pizza!" the rest of the kids chanted. "Pizza!"

---

1. I have observed that goats will eat *anything* that's put in front of them – anything. So watch your fingers!

"All right. I'm going!" Mrs Goat said as she went out the door. "Remember, stay inside!"

"We will, Mum," Mikey told her. "We've had wolf drills at school and everything. We know what to do."

Mrs Goat felt better knowing that her children had been taught to protect themselves, so she trotted out to the driveway, hopped into her car and headed to town.

VROOOOOMMMM!

CHAPTER TWO
DANGER AT THE DOOR

Deep in the terrible forest, Mr Wolf was hungry. He hadn't eaten in a few hours. His stomach was growling so loudly that it scared birds away.

GRUMMMMMMBBBLE.

Mr Wolf took a big breath. *Pee-YOO.* He was so hungry and his stomach was so empty that he had the most rotten breath in the world. Even HE was grossed out by it!

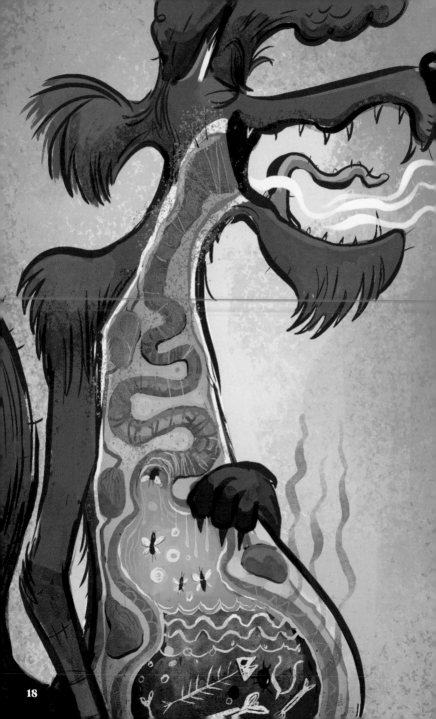

"Brush your teeth!" some unseen creature shouted from up in a tree.

Mr Wolf blushed. He couldn't help his bad breath. Instead he thought about where he could get food. Snacking on squirrels and mice just wasn't enough. And forget about rooting around under logs for bugs, slugs and millipedes. They did nothing for him, and they were slimy. He even thought about eating his own earwax, but he'd tried that before. He needed a meal.

 This is where things start to get GRIM. . . .

The wolf knew that right on the edge of the forest, Mrs Goat's house was filled with seven lovely, juicy, chunky little kids just ready to be gobbled up. As he thought about those goats, he started to drool. A steady stream of clear, sticky drool trickled from his mouth and hit the forest floor. The drool was so awful that it rotted the grass at the wolf's feet!

Before Mr Wolf set out to the Goats', he needed to sharpen his teeth a bit. After all, goats are tough. He got his file out and sharpened each tooth until it was as pointy as a pin.

Then he happily skipped out of his shack. He got his bike from the shed, and remembered to put some air in the back tyre. Mr Wolf pedalled down the path through the thick trees, singing a happy song to himself:

"Goats, goats, delicious goats.

I'm gonna eat those goats.

I'm gonna eat those goats!"

When he got to the edge of the forest, he parked his bike against a tree. Mrs Goat's car wasn't in the driveway. He could hear the kids inside, singing and jumping around. This was going to be a piece of cake. He'd eat them all up, and then he'd go home and take a nap.

He tiptoed up to the door. He turned the knob. It was locked!

"Fiddlesticks," the wolf whispered. Flinging the door open, running in and scaring his dinner before eating it was his favourite way to prepare a meal.

He knocked on the door. All noise inside stopped.

Finally, some hoofsteps clopped up to the door. "Who is it?" someone called from inside.

"AHEM!" The wolf cleared his throat. "It's your mummy," he said. "I've lost my keys! Won't you please let me in?"

"Your voice sounds weird," the goat said.

"I've got a sore throat," the wolf said. "You know, allergies. Hurry up and let me in. It's cold out here!"

Just then the wolf's empty stomach rumbled loudly.

BRRRRGGGGGHHHH!

"What's that noise?" asked the goat.

"Just a little gas," belched the wolf.

"Sounds like a fart to me."

"It's gas! Now open up and let me inside!" cried the wolf.

"If you're our mother, what are all our names?" the goat called.

Mr Wolf was stunned. He started making up names. "Lucretia, Giuseppe, Kiki, Mallory–"

"I knew it," the goat yelled. "You're the wolf!"

Mr Wolf heard a noise and looked up. A bucket hung from a string above his head.

"NOW!" one of the kids cried.

The bucket flipped over, emptying a dozen eggs on top of Mr Wolf's head. He brushed yolks and slime away from his eyes. Then he stormed away, stinky and sticky.

"I'll get those kids if it's the last thing I do," he snarled.

CHAPTER THREE
TROUBLE WITH GAS

"Those little pests," the wolf growled. The goats had seen right through his sore throat routine. They'd made a fool of him. He would have to come up with something good in order to trick them.

Suddenly he remembered something. Last year at his uncle Larry's birthday party, all the wolf cubs had changed their voices by sucking helium out of the balloons! The cubs' voices went super high, and they ran around singing silly songs. Helium would be just the thing to fool those goats![2]

He needed to get to the Party Shop and buy some balloons. He rode into town.

Mr Bison was behind the counter at the Party Shop when the wolf walked in.

"Good afternoon, sir. How can I help you?" Mr Bison said, looking at Mr Wolf suspiciously. He eyed a piece of eggshell dangling from the wolf's left eyebrow.

"I would like to buy twelve of your finest helium balloons," Mr Wolf replied.

2. It should be noted that sucking helium out of a balloon temporarily changes your voice by making sound waves travel faster than they normally do!

"Going to a party?" Mr Bison asked.

"That's none of your business!" Mr Wolf snapped.

"Well I never," Mr Bison huffed as he shuffled over to the helium tank. He filled up twelve balloons of all different colours. Then he handed them to the wolf, who was tapping his claws on the counter impatiently.

"Took you long enough," Mr Wolf said. He handed Mr Bison some money, took the balloons and stormed out of the shop.

Mr Wolf looked very funny riding through town on his bike with a dozen balloons floating behind him. Lots of townsfolk on the street stopped and laughed at him. The wolf didn't have time to think about that. He had a job to do.

As he turned a corner, he saw Mrs Goat loading several pizzas into her car. Steering towards her, he knocked the pizzas out of her hooves and onto the ground. Tin cans, earthworms, rotten eggs, napkins and cheese stuck all over her.

"I'm so sorry," he called as he pedalled past. He leaned over to pick up a slice of pizza off the ground. *Now she'll have to go back and get fresh pizza!* he thought, laughing. He had bought himself some time. Mr Wolf shoved the mud-covered pizza slice into his mouth. That would tide him over. He felt something squirming in his mouth and spat out a beetle. Then he swallowed the rest of the slice.

When he arrived at the Goats' house, Mr Wolf went up to the door. He sucked in a balloon and then knocked.

"Children, it's your mummy!" the wolf squeaked in his new voice. "I've lost my key, and this pizza is getting cold. Won't you please open the door?"

He heard the kids talking inside. Then everything was quiet for a moment.

"Who do you think you're fooling?" a voice finally came. "We can see your black paws under the door. Our mother has white hair. Go away!"

The wolf's stomach rumbled again.

GGRRRRRRRROOOOOOOOOOOO!

"And stop farting!" came another goat voice.

All the goats started laughing.

One of the balloons sprang a leak.

SQUEEEEEEEEEEEEE!

"Seriously, lay off the beans," another goat said, chuckling.

Mr Wolf stormed off and rode directly to the art shop in town. He needed some white finger paint.

 Ms Duck didn't trust Mr Wolf one bit. She refused to sell the paint to him.

"You sell me that paint, or I'll gobble you up!" Mr Wolf told her, opening up his jaws to reveal bright yellow teeth. The duck almost fainted. Not from fear, but because the wolf's nasty breath smelled so terrible. Trembling, the duck ran out the back to get the paint.

"I'm awfully sorry, Mr Wolf. We're out of white finger paint. I do have this vanilla earthworm pudding I brought for lunch. It has about the same colour," the duck offered. She held out a plastic container of shiny beige slime.

"I'll take it!" Mr Wolf cried, eager to get on with his plan. The duck took Mr Wolf's money as fast as possible.

As he was riding back to the Goats' house, Mr Wolf had another idea. He stopped at the Duffel Bunny Charity Shop and bought a pretty floral dress.

Mr Wolf was out of breath when he arrived at the Goats' house. He pulled the dress over his head. He dumped the beige pudding all over his paws. Finally, he grabbed one of the leftover balloons and crept up to the door.

Sucking in the helium, he knocked. "It's me, children! Let me in!"

They all looked under the door. There they saw white paws, not black.

"Hurry up! These pizzas are heavy!" the wolf called.

"Yay! Pizza, pizza!" the kids chanted.

Mr Wolf heard the lock on the door start to turn. He got ready to pounce.

CLICK!

As soon as the door opened, he jumped towards them.

"Fooled you!" he howled.

Before the goats stood the big bad wolf. His sharp fangs shone. His bad breath filled the hall with a yellow, stinky cloud. He looked hungry!

"What's with the dress?" Mikey Goat said.

"You look silly!" Tina Goat added.

"I thought it added a nice touch," the wolf said.

Then he remembered why he was there.

"I'm going to eat you all up!" he shouted. He growled and leaped inside the house.

CHAPTER FOUR

MR WOLF GETS HIS DINNER

"Scatter!" Tina Goat shouted to her brothers and sisters.

Mr Wolf tried to run after them, but he tripped on the dress he was wearing.

"ARGHHHHH!" he howled. He flailed and flapped, trying to get out of his costume. Globs of vanilla earthworm pudding flew all over. It was just the time the goats needed.

Alexander dived under the table.

Millicent scampered into the kitchen. She hid inside the rubbish bin.

Tina scrambled up the stairs to her room and got under her pile of hay.

David hid behind the toilet in the bathroom.

Alice jumped into the oven.

Leonard squeezed inside the vacuum cleaner bag.

Mikey was the youngest and the last to hide. He tiptoed to the giant compost bin and climbed inside. The smell of rotting vegetables made him want to go *MMMMMMM-MMMM!* He tried not to make a sound.

Meanwhile, Mr Wolf had finally untangled himself from that dress.

"What a bad idea that was," he said, tossing the dress aside. "Next time I'm going with a skirt and a blazer." He looked around and saw no goats.

"Ready or not, here I come," he snarled.

He ripped up furniture, smashed shelves and cabinets, and knocked paintings off the walls. He dumped out rubbish bins, overturned the cat's litter tray and flung food and rubbish everywhere. In the end he found Alexander, Millicent, Tina, David, Alice and Leonard.

The six kids cowered together in the corner.

"You know what happens next," Mr Wolf said impatiently. "Get in."

With that, Mr Wolf opened his mouth and pointed to it.

Defeated, they all jumped in, one after the other.

"You're mean," Alice said to him before she climbed in.

"Your breath smells like a dead cat," said Leonard.

"I think I'm going to be sick," said Millicent.

After the final goat was inside, Mr Wolf licked his lips in satisfaction.

"That was pretty easy after all," he said. He rubbed his belly and let out a loud burp.

"BEELLLLLLLLLLLLCHH!"

Mr Wolf stretched his arms, picked his nose and waddled outside.

Across the lane from the Goats' was a beautiful green meadow. Mr Wolf wanted to get home, but he was so tired. He dragged himself over to a big tree and passed out underneath it.

CHAPTER FIVE

MRS GOAT TO THE RESCUE!

Mrs Goat finally pulled into the driveway. After that rude cyclist had knocked her over, she'd had to wait for new pizzas to bake! This birthday party was not starting off well at all.

Balancing pizzas, she scrambled to the front door. She was about to put her key in the lock but found her door already open. She pushed it and went inside. Her entire house had been turned upside down!

"Kids?" she cried. She darted from room to room. Each room was worse than the last. There were bugs and rodents already picking through the wreckage.

She called each kid by name. None of them answered. When she finally got to the youngest, she had given up hope.

"Mikey?" she cried.

A sound came from the compost bin. "I'm in here, Mum."

Mrs Goat went towards the sound and helped her youngest kid from his hiding place.

"Mummy, Mr Wolf tricked us all," Mikey bleated. "We listened to what you said, I promise. But he changed his voice and his paws. He fooled us! And now all my brothers and sisters are gone! If I hadn't climbed inside that watermelon rind, he would have found me too!" He flung the half-eaten rind off his head.

Mrs Goat hugged Mikey. Then she stomped her hoof.

"That wolf messed with the wrong goat this time!"

She marched outside, planning to find him and drag him off to prison where he belonged. Little Mikey followed her out.

"There he is, Mum!" Mikey shouted. He pointed towards the meadow.

The wolf was sleeping under a tree. He snored so loudly that they could hear him all the way in front of their house.

"ZZZZZZZZZZZZZ*zzzzz* . . ."

They saw his full belly rise and fall with each breath. It was huge! It reminded Mikey of a giant dirty pink balloon with hair and pimples all over it. (And the wolf's belly button was an innie, which he never kept clean.)

Mrs Goat was crying as she raced across the meadow. This wolf had eaten her children. He would have to pay! She was about to clobber the wolf when she heard something.

"Who turned out the lights?" came a muffled shout.

Mrs Goat looked around. There was no one else nearby.

"Hey, let me out of here!" another voice came.

Mrs Goat couldn't believe her ears. It was the voices of her children. Could it be that they were still alive inside Mr Wolf's belly?

She leaned down and listened. Then she saw his stomach moving.

"He did swallow them whole," Mikey said to his mother. They watched kicks and punches going on inside Mr Wolf's belly.

"Oh my goodness," she said. "Run and fetch me my bag!"

Mikey trotted off to the house and brought the bag right back to his mother.

Now, as it turns out, Mrs Goat was the town's doctor. She knew just what to do to get her children out of Mr Wolf and keep him alive so he could pay for his crimes.

Here's where it gets pretty **GROSS**. . . .

Mrs Goat reached into her bag. She whipped out her white coat and threw it on. Then she took out a giant pair of scissors. She sliced right through Mr Wolf's stomach! The wolf was such a heavy sleeper that he didn't feel a thing.

SNIP! SNIP! A trickle of green sludge oozed from the cut.

She was careful not to hit anything inside.

Finally Mrs Goat pulled his belly open.

GURGLE! GURGLE!

"Here, hold this skin flap," said Mrs Goat.

"Gross!" Mikey shouted. "It smells like sick in there!"

"Shhh," Mrs Goat whispered. "You'll wake up the wolf!"

Mikey stood back. He held the disgusting flap of stomach.

Millicent popped out first. She was covered with pinkish slime and smelled horrible.

"Thank you, Mum!" she said. She joined Mikey.

"You stink!" he said to her.

The rest popped out one by one. Soon all Mrs Goat's children were safe and sound, even if they were all drenched in stomach crud and chunks of digested food.

"Now to sew him back up," said Mrs Goat.

"But what about the others?" Tina said.

"The others?" asked Mrs Goat.

Tina leaned into Mr Wolf's belly. "Come on out, everybody!"

Mrs Goat was surprised to see the Mackenzie kittens scamper out. Then came the Otter twins, Mr and Mrs Squirrel, the entire Raccoon family, six foxes, three chickens and two turkeys. Pink slime dripped from their bodies as they jumped up and down, happy to be free again.

All the town's citizens who had been missing were here!

"Goodness, how did you all fit in there?" Mrs Goat asked. She was about to sew the wolf back up, but she stopped.

"Wait a minute," she said to everyone.

"Let's teach this wolf a lesson. Everyone go and get something heavy and bring it back here right away!"

"Come on, sis," one of the Mackenzie kittens purred. "Let's go!"

They all scattered. Soon enough, they all returned, carrying giant loads.

Into the wolf's belly they crammed things.

Mr Squirrel put in some bricks. "I got these from a nice pig," he said as he clapped the dust off his hands.

Each of the goats put in a big stone, except for Mikey who put in a portable toilet.

The Otter twins threw in an anvil. The Turkeys hurled bags of rubbish.

The Mackenzie kittens donated their championship bowling balls. And a maths textbook. "It's very hard to digest," explained the kittens.

And then the Raccoons and Chickens arrived with a grand piano!

"Get this in there," they exclaimed as it teetered above the wolf.

Everyone jumped up and down on the pile. Once it was all packed in, Mrs Goat sewed him back up.

"This'll teach him a lesson he'll never forget!" she said, closing her medical bag.

Everyone was excited to see what would happen when Mr Wolf woke up. They hid behind a row of bushes and waited. And waited. And waited.

After a while, they saw Mr Wolf stir. He stretched and yawned and scratched his armpits.

"I'm so thirsty," he said, standing up and trying to walk. He was having trouble moving, and his stomach ached.

GRUMBLE! GRUMBLE!

"What's going on here?" he exclaimed.

He dragged himself over to the river. As he was getting some water, he saw all the townsfolk he had swallowed.

They were jumping up and down, pointing at him and laughing.

"Hey, wait a minute," he growled, feeling all the weight in his stomach. Then he sang a sad little song.

"What rumbles and tumbles

inside of me?

I know it's not goats,

but it sure is heavy!"

Then he fell into the river, and the current pulled him away.

Everyone thought he'd drowned until Mikey shouted, "Look!" The wolf had managed to come ashore on the other side of the river. He was so full of junk that he could never make it back to the other side.

Everyone in Mushroom Grove was safe! To celebrate, the town threw a giant party. There was pizza for everyone. They all sang happy birthday to little Mikey Goat.

And they all lived happily ever after! Even the wolf.

* * *

Months later, on the other side of the river from Mushroom Grove . . .

Mr Wolf decided he had HAD IT with hunting for food. He became a vegetarian.

He opened the first-ever meat-free restaurant for wolves. There they enjoyed soya-based versions of their favourite forest creatures, like Unsquirrel Nuggets, Pig-Free Porklet Sandwiches, SoyaGoat Nuggets and Cowless Burgers. All the things that had been sewn up inside his belly came out the normal way you get rid of your food. That piano – ouch!

THE END

COMPARING THE TALES

Benjamin Harper must have a stomach of steel. Why? Because it's hard to read his retelling of this grim Grimm tale without chewing some antacid tablets for your digestive system. Oof!

A grand piano? Bowling balls? An anvil? In the original story, the kids put heavy stones inside their furry enemy, but Mr Harper clearly decided that stones were not a big enough punishment! Besides, Harper's seven kids are funnier and cleverer than the ones in the Grimm story, so of course they would come up with some crazy and gruesome ingredients. You probably wouldn't accept an invitation to dinner at Harper's house!

Mrs Goat is away from home when the wolf attacks in both versions. But the pizza delivery chicken, the wolf's fancy dress, the helium balloons and the confused Mr Bison all come from Harper's delirious brain. How about the part when the wolf sings: *"I'm gonna eat those goats. I'm gonna eat those goats!"*? A ridiculously simple song, but that makes sense. The wolf is not a very clever villain, and the song shows exactly how ridiculous he is. Anyway, you've learnt something very important from the wolf's behaviour – if you have to suck helium and wear a dress before you eat, then maybe you should skip dinner!

GLOSSARY

ashore on or to the shore or land

blazer coloured jacket worn by sportspeople or schoolchildren as part of a uniform

disguise hide by looking like something else

flailed moved wildly

helium lightweight, colourless gas

satisfaction feeling of being content because you have done something well

scampered ran lightly and quickly

squirm wriggle around uncontrollably

stunned shocked

untangled removed knots or tangles

vegetarian someone who does not eat meat

wilted drooped

GROSS

BELCH let out gases in your stomach through your mouth with a loud noise

COMPOST mixture of rotted leaves, vegetables, manure and other items that are added to soil to make it richer

DROOL spit that drips from the mouth

EARWAX yellow or orange substance made inside the ears

PIMPLE small, raised spot on the skin that is sometimes painful and filled with pus

RIND tough outer layer of melons, citrus fruit and some cheeses

ROTTEN gone bad or decayed; something that's rotten usually smells horrible

SLIME slippery substance released by some animals

SLUDGE wet, muddy mixture

DISCUSS

1. The seven kids have to hide from Mr Wolf in the house. Imagine you're one of the kids. How would you feel when Mr Wolf made it into the house?

2. Mr Wolf tries to hide his voice and change his appearance to get the kids to let him in. What are some other ways he could have disguised himself?

3. Mrs Goat leaves the kids behind to go and get pizza. Talk about how different the story would have been if she had taken the kids with her. Would the wolf still have attacked them?

WRITE

1. The goat kids like having lots of gross toppings on their pizzas like the Rubbish Special. Imagine you're one of the kids, and write a list of your own gross pizza toppings.

2. Mikey Goat's birthday didn't go quite as planned. Imagine you're Mikey Goat. Write a diary entry about what happened during the day.

3. At the end of the story, Mr Wolf decides to become a vegetarian and stop trying to eat other animals. Write a version of the story where he tries to convince the Goats to try food at his new restaurant.

AUTHOR

BENJAMIN HARPER has worked as an editor at Lucasfilm Ltd and DC Comics. He has written many books, including the Bug Girl series, *Obsessed with Star Wars* and *Rolling with BB-8*. He lives in California, USA, where he gardens, keeps butterflies and collects giant robots.

ILLUSTRATOR

TIMOTHY BANKS is an award-winning artist and illustrator from South Carolina, USA. He's created character designs for Nike, Nickelodeon and Cartoon Network, quirky covers for *Paste* magazine and lots of children's books with titles such as *There's a Norseman in My Classroom* and *The Frankenstein Journals*.

PHOBIA

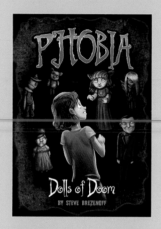

PHOBIA

Dolls of Doom
BY STEVE BREZENOFF

PHOBIA

The Creeping Clown
BY JESSICA GUNDERSON

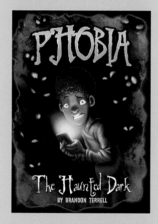

PHOBIA

The Haunted Dark
BY BRANDON TERRELL

PHOBIA

The Monster in the Mirror
BY ANTHONY WACHOLTZ

raintree

a Capstone company — publishers for children